Alphabet Birds

by

Philip A. Terzian

Bellingham Publishing

Alphabet Birds / by Philip A. Terzian. Photography by Philip A. Terzian

First Bellingham Publishing printing. September 2007

$ 20.00   USA

ISBN: 978-0-9798163-0-7

Printed in Hong Kong

To Erin and Janna,
my lovely daughters.

— P.T.

Avocet

A is for Avocet

A pretty smart bird
Is the agile Avocet
Stands on his right foot
So his left won't get wet

Blackbird

B **is for** Blackbird

The Blackbird's all black
Or so it is said
Except for his wing
That also has red

Cormorant

C is for Cormorant

The majestic, handsome Cormorant
Almost never sings
But stands upon the coastal rocks
And spreads his drying wings

Dove

D is for Dove

The soft, gentle cooing
Of the gray Mourning Dove
Announces to the world
That she's very much in love

Egret

E is for Egret

Look over here
Look over there
But whatever you do
Don't look at my hair

Flamingo

F is for Flamingo

Hey look at me
With my little red knee
I could stand on one leg
Since I hatched from my egg

Goldeneye

G is for Goldeneye

Can you please tell me why
I have such a silly name?
Could it be my yellow eye
That brought me such fame?

Hummingbird

H is for Hummingbird

Hummingbird, hummingbird
Hungry is he
Stopping for lunch
At the orange juice tree

Ibis

I is for Ibis

Skinny long legs
And a slender long beak
It all works just right
For the food that I seek

Junco

J is for Junco

My little black head
My little brown wing
I'm quite a dashing fellow
And you should hear me sing

Kingfisher

K is for Kingfisher

I have just one wish
While sitting on this twig
That when I catch a fish
I hope it's not too big

Loon

L is for Loon

Can you think of a word
That rhymes with loon?
How about dune?
Or moon, tune or prune?

Mockingbird

M is for Mockingbird

The Mockingbird sings
Whenever it's light
And he sings just as loud
All through the night

Night-Heron

N is for Night-Heron

She sits still as stone
To avoid being seen
But don't let her fool you
Her senses are keen

Owl

O is for Owl

My big yellow eyes
Let in lots of light
Makes it easy for me
To see well at night

Pheasant

P is for Pheasant

It's not too hard to spot me
Even in bad weather
Just look for my white neck ring
And my lengthy tail feather

Quail

Q is for Quail

All of my feathers
Lie in their place
Except for the one
That hangs in my face

Rooster

R is for Rooster

If you listen to the farmers talk
Some say that I'm plain homely
But if you ask my rooster friends
They'll tell you I'm quite comely

Swan

S is for Swan

The elegant long-necked Swan
So full of beauty and grace
Inspires love and kindness
With her gentle, peaceful face

Teal

T is for Teal

Her plumage like cocoa
It's the Cinnamon Teal
She paddles around
Hunting a meal

Upside-down Pelican

U is for
Upside-down Pelican

I have to turn my head around
When I first get out of bed
So I can scratch this awful itch
Atop my silly head

Vulture

V is for Vulture

This sharp-eyed, soaring bird
With an unattractive head
When he looks into a mirror
All he sees is wrinkly-red

Woodpecker

W is for Woodpecker

Acorn Woodpecker
That's his name
Pecking all day
That's his game

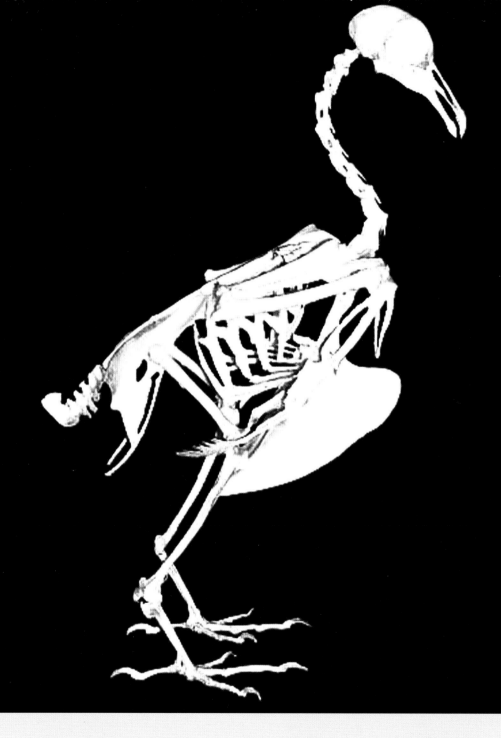

"X-ray Bird"

X is for X-ray Bird

Just like many animals
And little kids like you
It's not all that surprising
That we birds have bones too

Yellowlegs

Y is for Yellowlegs

I'm really not too colorful
Mostly white and gray
Except, of course, for my legs
Yellow like a sunny day

"Zebra Bird"

Z is for Zebra Bird

So eager was this little bird
To find and eat some seed
He didn't see the bright red sign
Or else he couldn't read

Phil Terzian was born in Schenectady, NY in 1952. He has a fulfilling career as an electrical engineer and also enjoys pursuing his interests in nature photography, astronomy, writing, wine making and kayaking. Phil has published several articles in aviation magazines and has had two portfolios of astrophotography images displayed at the Smithsonian Air and Space Museum in Washington, DC. Phil makes his home in Cupertino, California

About this Book

This book of colorful photographs and rhymes will entertain, educate and fascinate youngsters with the natural world of birds that is all around them. To encourage their questions and comments, each rhyme is written so that it relates specifically to the image on the facing page. A perfect bedtime book for parent and child to enjoy together, or for an older child to read alone.

The photographs in this book were taken using the Canon 10D and 20D digital SLR cameras with a variety of Canon lenses. The majority of the photographs were taken in the San Francisco Bay area. The "Zebra bird" (actually a Steller's Jay) was created using photo editing software. The bird never actually walked into the fence, nor was he painted.